The Gospel of Doubt

The Gospel of Doubt

Selected Poems of
Simon Bar-Jonah

Methow Press
Twisp, Washington 98556

© 2021 Greg Wright

Published by Methow Press

P.O. Box 1213, Twisp, WA 98556
https://www.methowpress.com

Printed in the United States of America

ISBN 13: 978-1-7366537-0-8

Cover image and interior art © Zoe Prince. Used by permission.

for those becoming

Contents

Let those who have eyes read
My journal is not the good news
My words will never save anyone

These are the collected poems of Simon Bar-Jonah, also known to history as Simon Peter. Culled from the hundreds of complete verse and fragments extant, these most "finished" works span the years of Simon's apprenticeship with Jesus of Nazareth.

As is typical with composers of verse, the poet often writes in the voices of other men, women, and even demons; for that reason, the effect is more that of an anthology than a monograph. The verses range from the arch and reflective to the apocalyptic and comic.

You will not encounter here the sanitized saint of stained-glass windows and hagiography. These are the words of a deeply troubled man struggling with brokenness and pride, and encountering a kind of holiness completely outside his prior experience. And he would also likely observe that the Jesus with whom he walked was outside all our experience, as well.

Greg Wright
Winthrop, Washington
October 2020

Prologue: On the Spit

and he came to the shore
while the crowd pressed in
and nets were being cleaned

And he espied two boats
two empty boats on the spit
boats being readied for the catch

And leaving the crowd behind
he waded into the shallows
turned and gazed upon me

Later there would be teaching
Later there would be fishing
Later there would be questions

Later there would be a catch
a legendary catch and nets straining
Later would be talk of sin and of hope

Later would come healings
and preaching and stories
tales of wrongdoing and wrongs righted

Later the crowds would adore him
Later they would mock and spit
Later—and much too soon—would he die

But now he chose a boat: my empty boat
Water dripped from his foot as in he stepped
and the boat rocked gently on still waters   ⳨

Addict

Unworthy

You don't want to know me;
I am just like you.

I am wonderfully made,
or so I have learned,
knit finely together.

But that was long ago,
and I am rent.
Who will mend my net?

I long for the refiner,
for the fuller's lye.
My talents are impure.
My linen is soiled.

I must be purified;
the kingdom of God is at hand.

I know that my redeemer lives,
but when I meet him,
what will he see?

A shredded seine.
My filthy rags.
A heap of slag.

He will turn away, just
like you.

I don't want to know him   ⊕

Career Day

I cast my net upon the waters
It makes not so much a splash
As a hiss
Each joined knot clutching feebly
At the surface as it plunges
Into the depths

This is what I do
What I do is who I am

Brother with brother
Son from father
Generation unto generation
We fish and we spawn
They spawn and we fish

And we never seem to get better

Ah! another empty net
We are not very good fishermen

But we do talk a good catch
What else can I do?

Ex Nihilo

What have we to do with you?
Our skin crawls, bristles, blisters.
Shrieks well from within our spine,
gall and wormwood in our bones.
Before we see you, we know you're there.

We know who you are—
the dreaded and bloody lamb,
anointed wielder of the sword,
bane of your bastard brethren:
the Holy Terror of God.

Have you come to destroy us?
Nothing is as it seems:
eternal, silent and cold—
sinister and lovely.
Yes, take it from us.

What can you do to us
that we have not done ourselves?   ☦

Now Wounded

We found him on a hillside, alone.
Somehow, I haven't a clue,
he lost himself in the crowds,
that feeding frenzy of agonizing hope.

The others told me the stories,
what he had done at Cana
with the wine and the Roman boy,
his words to Nazareth's rabbinim.

But I would still not believe,
had I not seen with my own eyes,
what he has done this day—
what he did for your mother.

I'm not sure I'm ready for this.

I used to please you so easily—
fistfuls of weeds were bouquets,
scrawls on a slate sonnets,
my first catch a blessed feast.

But soon after I became your man
my best was no longer good enough.
Now when I return, I see it in your eyes:
another day, another disappointment.

Can I tell you what I feel?

I saw the way you looked at *him*.
She rose from your bed, healed—
and she wasn't just grateful;
she wasn't just fever-free.

She was *enamored*. I saw it in her eyes:
This is a man worthy of my daughter.
You would have done anything for him.
You honored him without reserve.

Now I speak blasphemy:

This is how I want you to look at *me*.
This is the respect I want in my own home.
I want to do the things he does—
I want that kind of power, and more.

I want the throngs pressing,
that look in their eyes,
my name on their lips,
awe and reverence in their hearts.

Dare I say it? To be worshiped.

But that isn't me. It's him.
And what does he do? Slips away, hides.
When we found him— Yes, I begged his return.
He just looked at me, and smiled.

I don't understand
He's lost me
I fear
I've lost you   ✛

Panem et Circenses

Well, the Jesus Freaks came to town this week,
  And in case you didn't know:
We're the blokes you see up from Galilee
  With the lepers all in tow...

It's an age-old scam, and ain't worth a damn
  But you see it quite a lot:
Plant a shill in the crowd (or two! it's allowed)
  Then "heal" 'em on the spot!

We swear it's all real! This ain't no cheap deal—
  If Jesus you receive,
He'll touch you real light, then give back your sight.
  He will! You just gotta believe!

Cuz this you must know: He ain't in it for show;
  He's a very humble man.
He'll heal you, but: you must keep your mouth shut.
  Don't tell others, you understand?

The best way, you see—now listen to me!—
  To keep your profile low
Is performing great deeds and meeting "felt needs."
  It's obvious, ain't it, tho'?

Yet Jesus demurs and all glory defers—
  The reluctant Ringmaster, he.
After eight dozen pops, we're at the next stop...
  And he still hasn't charged a fee!

But I am no dunce—I saw the Cirque once
  On a visit to Caesaree:
You can keep a crowd long with free food and a song
  But to reap 'em, the show must repeat!

Yes, we've made a few friends, but where will this end?
  We can't hold the skeptics at bay.
Entertaining? Enough! But it's dangerous stuff—
  Such magnificent games we play!   ⊕

Center Ring

It gets worse.

I stood by the wall,
watched, arms
crossed. Sweat
rolled
down my calves.

He sat with the word,
taut, eyes
bright, spirit-
filled,
power upon him.

The scribes listened,
learnèd ears
closed, long
deaf,
with doubt teeming.

Crowds I know:
masses of people
pressed, hosts
sick
with desperate lives.

But this was new,
unmatched, not
foreseen: one
great
mystery to behold.

For the sky
fell, the roof
caved in,
commanding:
Pay attention.

A fragment of plaster upon my sleeve,
Disturbing my ennui.
What manner of message is this for me?
What portent from heaven?

But no great mystery to be revealed:
A mere hole in the roof—
A litter is lowered, a man inside,
Come with faith to be cured.

He forgives the man's sin!

Scribes shook heads,
muttered, not
believing, thought:
Blasphemous!
Worst suspicions confirmed.

He looked in their minds,
knew thoughts,
called them
evil.
Called me, too.

As a sign, he then
said *Rise*
and walk,
healed.
Which power is greater?

I cower inside,
known—I
blaspheme, I
suspect.
Can I be saved?

What reason have I?
Doubt? Or
belief? Both
warring
within my soul.

I have done no hard
work, haven't
sought. I am
fearful.
Why did he come to me?

I am
paralyzed.
Heal me, Lord.   ☦

Lambentation

This, Lord, is my shepherd?
   What does he want?
He bade me recline
   with tax collectors.
He led me into a night
   of loud drinking.
He confuseth my soul.

He crosseth my path
   with that of the unrighteous.
For heaven's sake!

I have walked through the valley
   of the shadow of sin.
And I, too, am evil:
   I fear being with him.
His rod and his staff—
   they bludgeon me.

He prepareth a table for me
   in the company of the unclean;
He anointeth my head
   with burning embers;
My mortification overfloweth.

Surely traitors and harlots will follow him
   all the days of his life.
And I shall remain
   unworthy and soiled.
Forever. ☦

Confession

On Sunday
I walked away from God
And opened an old wound
Peeled back the scab
Tugged at the ragged edges
Smeared the gore across my skin
And, good Lord—
Thrust in a dagger
Relished the pain.
Ah, woe is mine!
At the end of the day
I retired
Licking languidly
My safe and bloody harbor
Of resentment.

On Monday
I found a few neighbors
To talk with
And about.
We prodded and pried
Jimmied and jiggered
Meddled and muddled
Needled and nattered
Diddled and dirtied
Coddled and curried
Bantered and bandied
Sullied and soiled.
Oh! what fun we had.
Words flying furiously
Carefully carelessly
Delightfully damaging.
It feels so good to create.

On Tuesday
I slept late.
Okay, very late.

On Wednesday...
Now, what did happen
On Wednesday?
Ah.
I manufactured an earthquake.
Here is the recipe.
    3 c imagination
    1-1/2 c vanity
    1-1/2 c theatricality
    Dash of ill humor
    1 clove spite, crushed dry
    1 tsp leaven of Pharisee
    1/2 tsp cream of Tartarus
    2 tbsp rancid bile
    1 warped mirror
Mix dry ingredients thoroughly
After sifting imagination well.
Add bile and stir.
Let sit a while to rise
Until almost set.
Flatten mixture with a wooden mallet
And bake in the hot sun
Until it cracks
Like mud flats in the Negev.
Examine through warped mirror.
There.
You, too, can master the craft
Of finding faults
In just about anyone...
Including yourself!

On Thursday
Oh, on Thursday
I really enjoyed myself.
I believe I discredited
My entire family.
My cousin and I
Did scandalous things
In the wood behind the house.
You can just imagine.
Later, I tried to persuade
The neighbor girl
To flash me her privates
By telling her
"If you loved me, you'd show me."
She didn't bite.
Good for her!
In the afternoon
I tickled one of my best friends
So long and hard
She almost peed
My hands running
Not so furtively
Up and down
Over the satin smoothness
Of her tautly-bound breasts.
I think she enjoyed herself, too.
At least, I like thinking so.
Does this make you wonder
What else I did
On Tuesday?
No?
I really, really wish
I could remember
And tell you about that, too.

On Friday
Knowing the day of charades
Would begin at dusk
I indulged my appetite
For appetites.
May I say I gorged?
Thankfully I live
In a land of plenty
A veritable cornucopia
Of milk and honey.
In fact
I ate honeycomb with my honey.
We drank wine with our milk
And drank deeply
Wine from a round goblet
That overflowed.
I feasted on a heap of wheat
Set about with lilies.
I drank spiced wine
And the juice of pomegranates
Ran like hot grease
Over my chin
The fruit of my labors.
And it was good.
It was all good
Very, very good.
I was not sated
But I was satisfied
No! persuaded
That my lusts
Were scriptural.
I am my beloved
And I am mine.

On Saturday
I rested from all my wickedness.
I kept the Sabbath holy
Toeing the line neatly
Remembering that God
Also rested from his creativity
Recalling that I used to be a slave
Of some other dastardly master
Until God delivered me
Unto my bastard self.
And I rightly and crisply
Brought to mind
The Lord's command
To observe the Sabbath
And I kept it
Brutally kept it
A culmination of calumny.
I made no new wineskin
I mended no garment
I let the lost sheep die
I healed no one
Certainly not myself
I lit no lamp in the darkness
I milled no wheat in my palm.
Yes, I kept the Sabbath
I brutally and ruthlessly kept it
Shackled and tied it
Thrashed it soundly
Threw it into a pit
And sent it into bondage
All for the price
Of the bowl of red meat
I call another week
Another six-day indulgence

One more creative vacation from God
Followed by a septic
Sabbath from myself
Disingenuous

And holy.

Nay, it never be so.   ☦

Form Letter

Dear Applicant,

Thank you for your interest
in joining our glorious, elite
and ill-defined venture.
We are sure you will somehow
manage to make a great asset
of yourself in our company.

Space is limited! Act now!
There is, as you well know,
only so much room on a boat
or in a hillside hollow.

We are at present recruiting
a dozen or so men of Israel
who have already demonstrated
a notable capacity for following,
failure to follow through on jobs,
and remarkably little else.

It appears that this profile
fits your skills and experience!
We invite you to join us today
at almost the eleventh hour
for a detailed training lecture
with your fellow applicants.

We expect that there will be
a bit of rancor and quarreling,
a raised voice here and there,
even bragging and competition...
a ruckus in the marketplace,
as one might say.

But you will be pleasantly surprised
at what you are called to do
and are capable of doing...
Not to mention with whom!

No longer will you be
a disappointment to friends,
a reproach to family
or to self.

In no time at all
we will make you
a tax-collector of men.

Thank you for your kind attention,

Jesus   ☦

The Dream

The Lord brought me to Tabor,
To the mountain of Galilee,
And the elders were there—
The wise and the sage,
The foolish and the proud,
Along with a host,
All the tribes of the King.
The sun rose upon every one,
And when the afternoon rains came
Not a soul was spared.

And the word of the Lord
Rose up from the ground,
Rose up like a city,
Like a great city with towers
And battlements and courts,
Courts of a great temple
In honor of the Almighty.
The word of the Lord
Was a great city,
The city a kingdom,
An ancient kingdom rising up
From a mighty promontory,
A vast dais of three sides,
A solid foundation of stone
Thrust above the flood,
Far above the depths of time.
The Spirit hovered over the waters.

I saw the word of the Lord,
And the word formed words—
Words within the word.
And I saw the words
As they rose up,

And the words spoke as I watched,
The words rising up from a scroll,
Speaking with their own voice—
The voice of the Lord,
Words from my youth
And from the sands of time.

The elders listened—
The sage and the fool—
As the words rose and spoke.
I know not what the words were—
What others might say of them later—
But this is what I heard
From the words of the word,
From the mouth of the Lord.

The Spirit of the Lord is upon me—
   Good news for the poor.
Behold! the favorable year of the Lord—
   Good news for those who mourn.
The tongue of the Lord speaks justice—
   Good news for the meek.
The covenant of the Lord endures forever—
   Good news for doubtful souls emptied by the world.
The sacrifices of the Lord are a broken heart—
   Good news for the merciful.
The Earth is the Lord's, and all it contains—
   Good news for the pure in heart.
The Lord's angel pitches camp around His people—
   Good news for those who pursue peace.
The presence of the Lord is not far off—
   Good news for those despised and ridiculed.

Rejoice and repent
For we wake not from this dream!
The anointed of the Lord is at hand—
Good news for all the nations.

Our redeemer lives, God with us.
His name is Savior, seed of Abraham.
And his sandals tread lightly on the hills
Of a people who contend with God.   ☦

A Salt on the Senseless

The Spirit's upon him—
    But what about me?
For Him it's "fulfillment."
    For me, it's obscene.

He says we bring flavor
    To blandished, bare Earth—
A day of abundance,
    A season of mirth.

But I know what I bring:
    A hand without thumbs—
A jot without tittles,
    Percussion *sans* drums.

Something tasteless this way comes.

When I give my own brother
    Good cause for a grudge,
When I bare my false witness
    In front of the judge,

When my appetites drive me
    Instead of food's flavors,
When I withhold some kindness
    From those the Lord favors—

Something tasteless this way comes.

When I give *my* words weight
    Invoking God's name,
Or think *I* can decide
    Who's worthy of shame—

When I think of divorce
    As common, not rare,
Or retain for myself
    What God means to share—

Something tasteless this way comes.

If I hide a great city
    In a pit miles deep,
If I seek my own blessing
    While others yet weep,

If fears for tomorrow
    Throw doubt on today,
If I walk by His side
    But get in the way—

Something tasteless this way comes.

When the Lord brings me lambs
    Whom I treat like pigs,
Or when I am content
    With thorngrapes and thistlefigs,

When I think He can't meet
    My primary needs
While I nurture and cultivate
    My own grimy Phariseeds,

When I bet the impossible
    Simply *cannot* be done—
Something tasteless indeed
    This earthly way comes.

✠

Credo

The question came up, like yesterday's vomit:
What do I think of the "faithful" centurion?
Well, *he* believes the Master can heal;
I believe I am going to be sick.

They say he built the local school;
the city's elders find honor in that.
But even a temple-building despot
is still, I believe, a reeking despot.

The Romans are all insufferable heathens
who do abominable things with their "boys."
If he believes that he is unworthy,
I believe he likely has cause.

If he and his servant-boy suffer indeed
they probably reap what they've liberally sown.
The two are Gentiles, decidedly unclean—
I believe the worst, and am justified fully.

"Let it be done," the Master decreed,
"to you as you have believed in your heart."
Jesus healed what I would reject.

I believe I have much to learn.   ✠

Acolyte

Faith to Enter Nain

Did we not ascend to the hill with the Master?
Did we not stand in his holy presence?
But my hands are unclean and my heart is impure.
My lips are stained with falsehood, my vows with deceit.
This is the generation of those who seek him.

    Lower your heads, O gates,
    And be thrown down, you ancient doors.
    A procession of the dead issues forth.

What is death that it should swallow us whole,
that the shrill darkness of night should prevail,
that the grave should wound with its sting?

The dead pray not for healing, and corpses do not fast.
The shrouded ones have no use for sackcloth and ash.
What sacrifice can hands bring when they are cold?
Yet even these shall receive blessing from the Lord—
yea, righteousness from the God of their salvation!

    Yes, be lifted up in the city gates:
    throw yourselves wide, and open at the door—
    the King of Glory is at hand!

    Who is this king, the Lord of Hosts?
    He who will overcome death for all time,
    even the veil stretched out over all nations.

For the widow's son lives, and justice is served—
mercy reigns, and God visits his people.
Words from the Master's mouth are truth, and life.
His hands hold healing, and his heart compassion.
Yes, arise, young man! Your generation is made new.

Elegy for the Baptist

Dance for us, oh Lord
Step sprightly on the earth you wrought
  Lift your hands to the stars
To the lights you spread in the firmament
  Gird your loins and leap
Rise up to the tops of the trees you named
  Above the oaks of Mamre
Over the crowns of towering Lebanese cedar

Sing for us, mighty one
Lift your voice in an ancient stately tune
  Let your harmonies swell
Like songbird and raptor trilling as one
  May your low notes roll
Thunder crashing as waves burst upon stone
  Accompanied by your instruments
By rain and wind, infant's laugh and mother's cry

Sing for us, Jehovah
Sing for *us*
  By no means sing for yourself
Omit your primeval tune
  Speak not through angels
Who shine too bright
  Nor through prophets
For they offend

Yes, dance for us, God
Sway like reeds in the Jordan's marsh
  Move for us as we expect
And do not surprise us in the very least
  Follow our lead, master
Please us as we please ourselves
  In no wise be extraordinary

For the word is so hard to spell ☥

Doing the Math

I gazed at a candle through dark of night—
  'Twas a light of my own creation.
At first the flame surged high and strong,
  A flick'ring conflagration.

The hours drew on; the wick burned down.
  Wax melted from the heat.
As the fuel rose, the flame waned dim,
  Bedrown'd in its liquid seat.

What does it mean to be poorly wicked?
  Or wax with a pow'r too great?
Of what am I made? What does light reveal?
  A strength that must needs abate?

I keep stumbling over such troublesome thoughts,
  Yes, stumbling over again:
The yoke may be easy but the ploughing is rough.
  My patience is wearing thin.

The fruit of one's labor, the learnèd ones say,
  Shall vindicate hearts of wisdom.
Shed light on my deeds, and what can be shown
  But vindictive interdiction?

Bethsaida, Capernaum, Chorazin—yes,
  I fancy I'm better than that.
But am I wisdom's child? I hardly think so.
  I'm more like a fool's bastard brat.

And yet I am greater: I have seen, and repent—
  Even know that "greater" means "less."
But how would I rate against Sodom and Tyre?
  Oh, yes—it's an odd calculus.

If I pour out my wax, I burn bright once again,
  My flame leaping high and alive.
But how can this be, when my burden is light?
  It seems I must die to thrive.

Whose Name I Wear

lamb it is
yes lamb
I catch a scent
also of fennel
fennel and cumin

my tears flow
and there is also
the odor of perfume
of nard and precious
oils which mingle
with my tears
my dark curls
wet

oh my love
you know me
look on me now
and despise
slander me
to your honorable guest
have I not sinned
enough to please you

yes
well you know me
how else could I have
darkened your door
this sacred night

does the teacher know
the things I do
for you

and for the other
man in this room
who breaks bread
with you
and dips lamb
in your dish
the man who shares
your name
your cup
your woman
your secret sin

you have both dipped
deeply and far
too often

yes my tears flow
as I bathe
the teacher's feet
as you have never
bathed his
or mine
yes deign touch
all else
save my feet

oh this is a sweet
and bitterly pleasing
sacrifice

I shall forgive you
as the teacher has forgiven
my surfeit of shame
his eyes tell me
I have sinned
enough for him

so I shall forgive you
your deceit
your holy hauteur
your conviction
that there is a pure
way to be puerile

yes there is lamb
and you may eat
let the fat fennel and cumin
dribble in your beard
as you gape
dumbfounded
at this teacher
who honors this whore
above his host
who has much
too much
to learn

yes I shall forgive you
when the tears
no longer fall
as I shall forgive the other
Simon too
the one the teacher calls
the rock

whose name
would he rather
wear tonight
do you think

yours
or mine
or another's

⳨

Yon Holy Mess

What do you feel, Mary? What runs through
Your mind when an unclean spirit leaves,
When a demon abandons its hold on a man?

    the void is more potent
    than the power which flees

You know this to be true, don't you? True for you?
You have been healed more than once.
The first demon went out, seven returned.

    more of your own evil
    self will never suffice

What were the seven cast out from you, Mary?
Do you know? What were your many torments?
Tell us, can you name them one by one?

    I know them not, but these
    seven I should never desire

    One that speaks from the place of darkness
    One indifferent to words of the wise
    One too proud to confess and repent
    One consumed with proof and doubt
    One that mistrusts the good it sees
    One that sooner divides than unites
    Or prefers an ordered void to a holy mess

    like mine   ☦

Hence the Harvest

Who is his mother?
Who are his brothers?
Who his father?

These call him insane
They wag the finger
And quote the psalm

Join not with the wicked
Nor fellowship with sinners
They are worthless as chaff

But see what fruit
These few have borne
What their seed yields

His brothers have never known him
The good news falls on hardpacked paths
They hear but they do not believe

His mother was a rocky place
That received the word with joy
Yet she of late has fallen away

Even he that was his earthly sire
Good soil indeed that once he was
Heeds him not due to worldly cares

But those with eyes may see
And those with ears may hear
Yes those with hands hold fast

These are his chosen people
Those who bear much fruit
In whom the word takes root

Praised be the Lord
There are many dawns
Before the harvest moon

Nothing is ever hidden
Except to be revealed
Another season awaits

A crop may be spoiled
By waves of driving hail
Or late summer drought

Judgment comes not yet
Tend to your own fruit
Husband your own fields

May the dormant seed
Await the wadi's flood
Or spade-turned earth   ☦

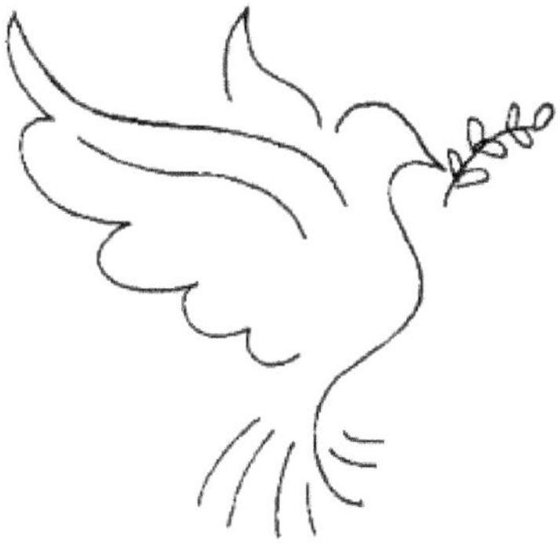

The Kingdom of Simon

What is the Kingdom of Heaven like?
To what may it be compared?

The Kingdom is a difficult knot
that may not be undone:

At one end of the rope is your ship
straining to run with the tide;
at the other end is a stubborn anchor
caught fast on a hidden reef.

Again, the Kingdom is a winding path
that doubles back onto itself:

At the crossroads you become confused
and travel the same way repeatedly.
The fifth time over a familiar stretch
you cry out to the heavens in frustration.

The Kingdom is also a strong headwind
pushing against your oars at dusk:

As you struggle homeward with a heavy catch,
it will rot, as you missed the market.
More, the Kingdom is a confusing psalm,
equal parts confession and calumny.

    Or, if you like, the Kingdom of Heaven
    is a thing I cannot understand,
    a patently obvious and noble truth
    that hides in the reeds at water's edge,
    a hungry nesting hatchling whose cries I hear
    but whose beak I only glimpse at feeding time.

I nod, and I say, "Yes. I see the bird."
I do not, and am ashamed of the truth.   ☩

Where Hope Lies

You can drown
In a cup
Of water
I have
Heard it said

I reflect
On this truth
As the bucket
Weighs my arm
Before I bail

The sea
Now calm
Casts an eerie
Pall, the shadow
Of the master

Falling upon me
As I crouch
In the bow
I trust
In the Lord

For protection
So why
Do I wish
To fly
To the shore

Because God sends
The rain
And the wind
And the waves
Of the storm

On the wicked
And the righteous
Alike as I
Have heard
The Master say

And I know
Not which
I am
So where
Is my faith

In the back
Of the boat
Lying down
Asleep and
Dampened.   ☩

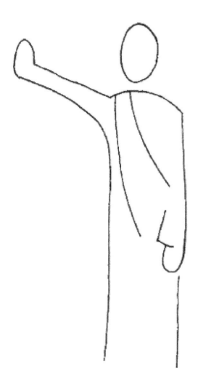

What I Must Be

I found the Lord
    On the Gadarene road:
        He came over from Galilee

I watched from the hill
    As I ate my lunch
        And lounged in the shade of a tree

As Jesus went by
    On his way to the town
        The lunatic stopped him cold

You know the one:
    A-raving and bare,
        About whom the stories are told—

He wails alone
    In the dead of night
        And harasses trav'lers by day

His lair is dark
    And his heart is black;
        He scares all the humans away

But not this morn—
    He said to the Lord
        The most incredulous thing

"What have I to do
    With the Son of God?
        What have I to do with a King?"

I didn't know then
But I do know now
That I am unworthy, unclean

For the spirit went out
Of that miserable soul,
Came out and left him, unseen

And found its way
Across the fields
And forced itself into me

Now I rush headlong
Down my Gerasene hill
To cast myself in the sea

You keep me safe
O Lord of hosts—
It is you alone who saves

I will be your swine:
I'll die to drown
The demon beneath the waves

Night Psalm

I have tested my thoughts
and examined my heart in the night.
I have scrutinized myself
and found bounteous wrong.

I cannot believe what I am about to say.

I have followed your commands
instead of cruel and evil men—
I need your help to stay on the path
as I waver from following you now.

I am praying to you, Lord,
because I know that I will hear you answer.
Bend down and listen as I speak—
by your mighty power grant safe harbor.

I have drawn nets from many waters—
yes, in many seas have I weighed anchor.
I have seen the reflection of Tabor
in the blue of Gennesaret at dawn;
I have seen the crimson moon rise
over the prow on Hula at dusk;
I have tasted alkali and dust
from the great Salt Sea on broken lips,
even felt the burst of the Cretan breeze
force its way through my robes off Joppa.

The storms have not cowed me—
the gales have never kept me from port;
neither rain nor sleet has chilled
and the waves have not dashed my spirit.
I have even stood by your side
at the most miraculous of calming seas.

But today we set forth
on a voyage I dare not make.
Guard me as you would guard your own
and hide me in the shadow of your wings.

Protect me from the spirits
in the waters off Gadara, Lord—
they would drag me down
and surround me in the deep.
They are like lions of the sea
waiting to devour my flesh—
I can hear my bones crack
as their fangs rend sinew and hide.

You are their undoing, Lord, and mine:
stand against them, for they are legion.

    Because I am chosen I will be at peace:
    when I awake, I will see you face to face.   ☦

Call & Response

        Twelve years have I bled,
        a gross of months remained unclean.
        No amount of hyssop may be of aid,
        no band of scarlet yarn bind this wound.

        Not soon shall I forget the burden I have borne.
        And even should the bleeding cease
        yet one more week shall I be put away.
        But of what import may those days be?

A dozen years have I lived to die,
your blood coursing through my veins.

The breath of the Almighty gave me life—
why now should I be afraid?

        Each morn when I arise, I arise unclean
        and the place where I have lain, defiled.
        No one may approach my bed and its taint.
        To raise a sheet is to share the curse.

        And through the day I dare not sit
        for if my child should take my place
        she must wash all that she wears
        and bathe, remaining unclean 'til night falls.

        Would my husband dream of lying with me,
        of joining with my flesh these dozen years?
        For seven days would he be set aside—
        because of me be cast from the synagogue.

Those who are older should have room to speak,
for with passage of years grows sage advice.

But the Spirit of God swells my breast
while the chests of the wise and learnèd sag.

I am a new wineskin, yet am about to burst.
Will you listen? Shall I tell you what I think?

> I did not ask for this,
> yet this blood remains.
> Twelve years have I bled,
> seven score months without relief.

> Yet find me pure, Lord.
> Test my motives and my heart.
> I trust in your promises
> and live according to your truth.

You and I belong to God; we both were formed of clay.
Dread not my words, and I shall not fear your touch.

So hear me: God speaks, and speaks to you now—
when you lie down, when you sleep, and as you wake.

Even should my deathbed cast shadows upon your soul
'tis the light of God that lies in wait.

> Count me not with those who choose evil
> or bind my fate with that of thieves.
> My hands are unclean, to be sure,
> but not with evil plans and schemes.

> I have not filled my days with wrong,
> set apart as I am from all that is wicked
> as well as from all that salves the soul.
> It is a foul holiness that I endure.

A messenger from heaven shall bear these words:
Rescue this one from the grave; be thou her ransom.

And you shall rejoin: God has received me with joy—
I have become as blameless as my child.

        Turn my way and lavish me with mercy,
        for I am isolated in my distress, Lord.
        Cast your eye upon my sorrow
        and bend your compassion upon me.

Look upon the stars—are they soiled by your flow?
Because I am clean, do they shine more brightly?

        I long to worship again in your presence,
        to find shelter in the Lord's sanctuary.
        To this end I dare to stand my ground
        and reach out to him as he passes.

Know only this—our hearts hear: Come, be with me.
And the blessed heart returns: Lord, I haste.

        Will the world end should I touch his cloak?
        Is my filth of more weight than his glory?
        Is my blood enough to mar the spotless?
        Or shall his power make me clean?   ☦

Credo Redux

"Let it be done," the Master yet declares,
"to you as you have believed in your heart."
Jesus heals again—but I no longer feel repulsed.
I believe Jesus has taught me a great deal.

I believe the rabbi calls me to be extraordinary,
and because he stepped into my boat I can be at peace.
I believe the King of Glory is in the city's gates.
My faith is no longer dampened, lying in steerage.

I believe that God will lead me safely over troubled waters.
I am not defined by the sins of the "other Simon,"
yet I believe I am still a mess—holy, but still a mess.
I know that I must mindfully tend to my own nets.

More of my own tattered sails will not deliver me,
yet my filth is not more weighty than God's glory.
I will be the Lord's swine if I must—but the Lord's!
This does not overwhelm me, is not too heavy to bear.

Yes, I have been scorned by those who hate me.
I have been despised by neighbors, mocked by friends,
and I have even been marginalized by my wife.
When cousins and aunts see me, they walk the other way.

But I believe in the Lord of Hosts
and I have put my future in his hands.
I believe the stage has been set
and the New Simon is ready to make a scene.

Yes, let it be done to me as I have believed.   ☦

A Letter Home

See with what confidence I write!
Hand over hand,
I was made for this work—
like setting sails.
I am a fisher of men!

I gave a blind man sight today,
and he was not the first.
Andrew and I are hauling nets
at the same rate,
moving light and fast.
We are saving souls from the depths
and sending demons down
bound with anchors.

I am alive at last.

Much of what Jesus told us
I cannot fathom—
talk of sheep, and of harvests.
But Mother!
Our nets verge on breaking!
There is no limit
to what we can do.

You say, *Wait!*
There must be a catch.
Yes, there must be—
and it is up to us now!
We have authority to cast nets
as we see fit into the sea
called Israel.

Lost fish throw themselves
into our nets
at the sound of our voices.

Yes, Jesus warned
that opposition would come.
The unworthy who reject us,
those who do not repent and follow,
will get what they deserve.
We will outfox the wolves.

I am not the least bit surprised
at what my hand finds to do.   ⊕

Less Than Learnèd

What would it cost to feed such a crowd?
What will it take to sate my soul?

On the one hand I've seen what the Master can do.
Yes, he must certainly increase—and multiply.

And divide.
So on the other hand...

There are only so many things I count on in life,
and I know what my larder can muster.

No, this did not feel like a test
as much as a trick question

of incalculable proportions.
We all can tell when things don't add up.

So what should we make of these leftover crusts?
What will I find when I sort through these orts?

Do we ever understand what we toss aside?
What is the takeaway from this objectionable lesson?

What am I left with at the end of the day?
5000 facts that cannot be grasped—

Two fishes and five loaves of doubt—
Twelve lame excuses for lack of belief—

and my basket of miraculous scraps.   ☩

A Miktam of Simon

Regarding the time when I sank into the sea but somehow convinced myself I was a hero. To be sung to the tune of "Do Not Destroy."

What would this trip be like
I wondered
Could I master crossing this sea
I wondered

Such nights used to be so exciting
Out on the water—to be free
But now my heart just starts pounding
Hey, what's the matter with me

I'm used to facing bad weather
I've done more than others dared
Now my spirit just seems tethered
Tell me—did I really feel scared

Our ghostly rabbi walking on the water
What's so fearsome about that

They can criticize me if they want to
They can talk behind my back
They all thought I played the jester
But I showed the courage they lack

I put my foot out onto the water
I made my way toward the Master
I didn't cower in the boat
So what if I didn't stay afloat

Oh, let them all call me a failure
I do better than their best
Jesus had the sense to put me to the test
And I made them see I have confidence in me

I know now I can impress them
They aren't fit to wash my feet
Even in their own blood, heaven help them
They now look up to me—admire me

With each step I became more certain
I would sink beneath the brine
But I had confidence such failures are just fine
You have to agree, I have confidence in me

I have confidence in sunshine
I have confidence in rain
I have confidence in brawn, if not my brain
And so you can see I have confidence in me

Strength doesn't lie in numbers
Strength doesn't lie in health
Strength is not afraid of making blunders
When you step out, step out! Which tells me

All I trust I give my heart to
All I trust becomes my own
I have confidence in confidence alone
Besides which you see I have confidence in me   ☦

Devil's Food for Thought

My record to date, I must clearly admit,
    Has not been so very grand.
When questions are put I most often confess
    That I simply do not understand.

But Jesus today taught a difficult bit
    And some of my mates took their leave.
So they walked away? I couldn't care less.
    I am not the least bit bereaved.

And here is the part that gives me great hope—
    This time I got what he meant!
I believe in my heart (and this is God's work)
    The Master's the one the Lord sent.

So much of the time I've been such a dope
    About teaching that goes over my head.
But I'll draw a line, and one I won't shirk:
    True life is true blood and true bread.

This passion consumes my soul but I think:
    How does one eat a king?
It's a hunger that looms over each waking hour,
    Over all the bounty God brings.

My spirit seeks bread and is parched for a drink
    Even as I sink 'neath the waves.
My arms are like lead and my bile is sour—
    But God reaches out and he saves.

So I shall ignore my small gnawing doubt
    And embrace this nugget of truth
And I'll ask for more—yes, more, if you please,
    Even if my entreaty's uncouth.

Yes, he is the Root the seers wrote about—
   The Holy One, Bread that Sustains.
This is a truth even demons will shout—
   It's a confession for which I'd be slain.   ♰

A Child's Garden of Vice

Now I sit me down to eat
And this old saw I shall repeat:
If my hands I have not laved
There is no way I shall be saved.

For through my mitts, begrimed by toil,
My soul shall also be made soiled.
This is fact—it's true, I know,
Because my teachers told me so.

And by this same fine way of thought
I won't be helping Mom a lot—
For if I "give it all to God"
There's naught for her. Ah, what a fraud!

But since you ask, I'm not so sure
Such rules have kept my motives pure.
I tend to seek what's best for me...
And that's what's best for *you*, you see.

But can I possibly believe
Such shams as this the Lord won't grieve?
The things one eats don't spoil the man—
That's all just crap, you understand?

Oh, yes—I see! My heart's the key!
It's not my gut shall set me free.
But Jesus says without a doubt
What God don't plant he'll sure root out.

I'm just not sure; what does this mean?
I thought that all green plants were clean.
There must be some that God will burn...
And they're the ones that *we* should spurn!

Postscript
  What did Jesus mean about
   The blonde leading the blonde?
   I didn't get a clear answer
    On that.   ☦

Revile Us Again

Listen, my brothers, to my instruction
As I bring you lessons from our past
Stories of what we have seen and heard
Truths, hard truths, we will not hide

So that those who come behind have no cause
To be like us, stubborn, rebellious, and ungrateful

Many of our brethren, even some of you
Walked away after the miraculous feast
Not comprehending the Lord's teaching
And forgetting all that he had done

That he had walked upon the very waves
That he stilled the storm and sea
He made wine flow from jars of water
Offered living water to those who were lost

Yet we kept refusing the rod of our shepherd
Not believing that he is our only bread and wine

Did he not feed the multitude
With just five loaves and two fish?
Did we not eat the food of angels
Even more than 5000 men could consume?

We took our fill, he gave what we craved
And while that taste is yet on our lips
We question him yet again, saying
What can you do now with seven loaves?

Are we destined to failure like our forebears?
How often will we test the Mighty One's patience?

Can we not recall his signs and wonders
How he healed the sick from afar
How he caused the deaf to hear
How he raised the dead in the city gates

And sent a herd of demons into the sea?
Did he not fill our nets to the point of breaking?

Yes, we are as faithless as our fathers
As undependable as an unpatched sail
And the Lord has sent us a sign
Because he is angry with his chosen ones

Our hearts rejoiced when Jesus named the heathen a dog
But they quailed when he gave her scraps from our meat

Yes, this is how the Lord will repay our treason
When we squander the bounty he spreads before us

It is one thing to marvel at a basket of scraps
And make light with a whimsical verse
It is another to hold each morsel as sacred
And jealously guard what the Lord provides

He has called us from our nets
From our tax-rolls and our scheming
And made us caretakers of his word
We shall never abandon him again

Yes, those who deny the Lord
Will cringe before him forever
Let us dine instead on the finest bread
Be filled with wild honey from this rock

Shall he feed us on sorrow
And shall we drink of our tears?
Shall wild animals feed on our fruit?
Or rouse we from our drunken slumber? ☥

Interrogative

How do you describe a tree
    To a blind man?
What do the words *tall*
    Green or *branch* signify?
How do you meaningfully distinguish
    Between shade and broad sunlight
    Between dappled rays and black of night?

"Take a thin bit of your darkness
And then imagine other bits
Of darkness coming off to left and right
With still other bits of darkness
Of a slightly different shade
Sprouting off or hanging
Pendant from those first bits and
Waving about
No, fluttering
No, just hanging"

Words fail us

As well say
A tree is a noun
Festooned with other nouns
That verb adverbly
In vibrant shades of adjective

Article is nice, aren't they?

And what does sight mean
    To a man born blind?
Verbal gymnastics become so much chaff
    Useless scales to be laid aside

Men are not trees,
    Nor like trees but moving about.
When you have finally seen a man
    Or a tree you know it

The Kingdom of God is not a metaphor
    Nor like a simile
Should we bow and scrape to an analogy?

As well say
The Kingdom of God is
A thin bit of your darkness
Verbed with vibrant nouns of adjective

This is the silence of darkness,
    The solo voice of your empty friend
Harmonizing with the melody of the Liar

When you finally see the light, you will know it.   ✠

Who I Am

The Lord is my rock
    My fortress and my savior
My God is my rock
    In whom I find protection

Lead me to the towering rock of safety

God is my refuge
    The rock where no enemy can reach
Yes, he is my father
    And the rock of my salvation

Let me trust him for he is my place of shelter

The Lord is good, my rock
    And there is no evil in him
Righteousness and justice
    Are the foundations of his throne

It shall stand from everlasting to everlasting

Yes, the Lord is my fortress
    The mighty rock where I hide
Let us shout joyfully
    To the rock of our salvation

He will judge the nations with his truth

And Jesus is this Christ
    The son of the living God
I, Peter, the Rock
    Confess this truth

And on this rock Jesus will build his church

Excellent

What's a church?   ☦

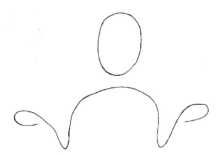

Matthew, Take Note

This is a test
This is only a test

Had this been an actual rebuke
I would not feel so strongly
That I am right

Like Phineas of old
I have had courage
To intervene

To say, Jesus, be encouraged
To know his pessimism is not prophecy
But a dark cloud, a mood that will pass

And I did not quote the psalm
To just wag the lip, or the finger

No
I am not ashamed

> Jesus, you will ascend to your throne forever
> Fame everlasting to all generations
> Now is the time to bring aid to your city
> To your people, who love even the dust of its streets
>
> You will restore to Jerusalem its glory
> For God has looked down from heaven with mercy
> Sending salvation to those condemned to die
> Yes, the name of Jesus will be praised in Zion

But he cut me off in mid-thought
Yes, Jesus lays the rebuke on me
Yet I am The Rock, no stone for stumbling

I am not Satan
This is only a test

And like a dark cloud
Or a dismal mood
I shall pass   ☩

All Things

All things are immanent

Time is an all-consuming fire
In which dwell Moses and the Prophet
I have seen light shine on their faces
And heard the voice of God

> How does one house Leviathan?
> Shall we erect three shrines for the blessed?
> Shall I encamp for a week in an olive-branched bower?

I have stood on holy ground
Yes, here is one in whom God is well pleased
Let a double share of that spirit fall on me

> Who shall join Elisha in the apocryphalyptic harvest
> To lead this final ingathering of the chosen?
> Shall it be our half-dozen duos of dimwits
> Joined at the ever-jabbering lip, less one
> The four brace of brotégés and the Glorified Three?

All things are immanent

And long have been, and shall be
All things burn, and shall continue to burn
We have entered the fire
And are not consumed

As I am, Moses was
And Elijah is
Jesus shall be

Forever   ♰

Fantasy of Misfiguration

And Moses came down from Hermon
    Robed in splendor and ire
    Graced by God

And the sound of the crowd
    Came to Joshua's ear
    The ear of the Servant's Right Hand

Moses inquired, *What is this we find?*
    Weak-minded golden-calf worship
    Wastrel works of the ineffective

Mere gilt bovinity cannot cast out a demon
    Cannot soothe the raging spirit
    No, cannot still a writhing body

Yes, Elijah came down the mountain
    Full of the Lord's might
    Elisha joining at his side

Impotent would-bes could not withstand him
    He girded his loins with leather straps
    And called down power from on high

Elijah's fire took the waters of unrest
    Consumed the blood and wood of torment
    Destroyed even stones of doubt

No, the boy is not dead
    Moses and the Prophet have delivered him
    Poured living water from the mountain

Man of God, even a king
    May not command you to come down
    So please spare our lives

Lord, your people are a stubborn lot
    For the sake of your glory be patient
    Do not destroy the faithless out of hand

Moses must depart from Nebo
    And Joshua shall part the Jordan

Elijah must be taken in fire
    And Elisha shall raise the dead

Joshua has been on the mountain, and prays
Elisha has been anointed, and fasts

The might of the Lord shall abide, in me   ☧

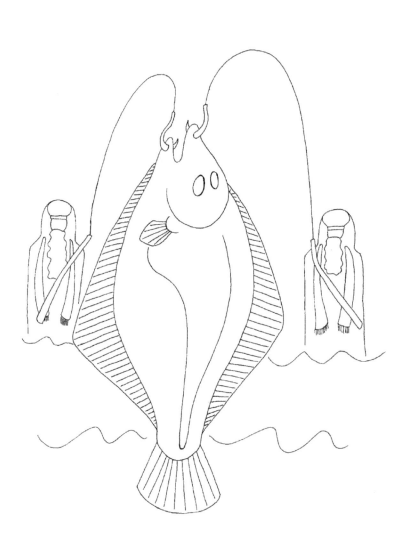

Poser

fetch to the sea for a sole
what, do you think, you are like to find in its mouth?
drachmae for the temple tax?

more like to find baited hooks
the Pharisees' tongue-traps for the Fisher of Souls
gill-nets for the gullible

but make no mistake about this
we shall give no offense and we shall pay the tax
and they shall pay too... oh yes

☦

Worst Things First

It was inevitable that I should come.
"Bring one of the children here," Jesus said.

So I brought the Lord our fellow John,
    But he was too fawning;
And I brought the Lord the brother James,
    But he was far too thundrous;
Andrew brought himself
    As he is so pushy;
Philip came after much thought,
    But he was too, well, grown up;
Matthew approached with interest, naturally—
    And Jesus found him calculating;
Judas was busy with his schemes,
The other Simon rebelled,
And Thomas... well, you'd call him
    Many things but never trusting.

But it was inevitable that I should also come
    And prove to be a stumbling rock:

    Lads and lasses, come to me!
    Yes, come singing and dancing!
    Come to my open, undespising arms!
    Cups of water, cool water for all!

    O, my brothers have offended me
    But I shall not bear a grudge! Not I!
    I'll forgive all ninety-nine—plus one!—
    Seventy-six—plus one!—times! Each!

Asks the psalmist:
    What if the Lord had not been on our side?
Ask I, the apist:
    What if we have not been on his?

Have patience with us, Master—
We shall repay all, as we have been repaid.

It was inevitable that I should come.
And I was the last.

Yes, I came last.
    Be mindful of that.   ⊕

Ode to Ministry

How wonderful and pleasant 'tis
    or so that I have heard
When brothers live in harmony...
    and walnuts split in thirds.

For harmony is near as dear
    as Aaron's 'nointing oil
That ran from top his balding pate
    and 'broidered garb did soil.

Yes, harmony is neat and sweet
    as lofty Hermon's dew
Bedecking grass in swardlets green
    that cattle just pass'd through.

Oh, brothers bait and brothers taunt
    they mock, and yes, so chide
That when to public 'vents they 'vite
    you're more inclined to hide.

And even those you call your own
    by choice if not by birth
Can be the source of much chagrin
    and barely stifled mirth.

Yes, let the dead inter the dead
    for that's what "brothers" do.
Make no mistake—If peace you want
    this min'stry's not for you!   ✢

United Affront

Jesus didn't show, did he?
Is it that he thinks he has
better things to do—or a
rendezvous with a demon?
Oh, but then he arrives this
morning, adds the misery
of chastisement that endures.
He'll keep it up—forever!

I know one thing—it is this:
he surely has a demon.
The Law of Moses endures;
it brings joy, not misery!
This is heart-truth, not what he
claims—mere appearance that has
fooled us all. We will find a
silence for him. Forever.

We cannot follow where he
goes? Well, who among us has
that desire? We want just this:
an end to his misery!
As well that he go to a
Greek as go to a demon.
This is a truth that endures:
division is forever.   ☩

The Wordless Wonder

It's hard to know what to write
    and would it matter if I did?

There's little use in visionaries
    with eyes clenched shut
Or for scribes who study not
    what they scratch with their quills

If you could read, would you say
    this book does not open to you?
If you could not, would you tell me
    you do not want to listen?

Yet the time is nigh in this broad darkness
    I have seen it plain as night
When those who play at being deaf
    will hear indictment writ in dust

For nothing speaks louder than silent shame
    and there's dirt enough to go 'round
Those who lift stones find their hands
    turned against themselves

Those who play judge and jury slink away
    at loss for word and wit
This is the day when the wise understand
    when the learnèd get schooled by the Master ☦

Dialogue

Follow, and walk not in darkness
For I am the Light of the world

    So say you of yourself
    You bear false witness
    For you know such does not count

Ah, but it does
And my witness is true
For a figure of speech gets at truth
But is not truth itself
And again, I am not one
But two, my father and I being one
A satisfying witness

    We know your father
    And where is he now?
    You are too clever by half

And you know not what you know
And know less what you do not
For you are of the halves
And I Am of the halved-not

☥

Apocalypse of Posteriority

(after Milius of Trestles)

Do you know the man really likes you?
Jesus *likes* you. He *really* likes you.
He's got something in mind for you.
Aren't you curious about that?

I know something you don't know.
Jesus is clear in his mind, but his *soul* is weary.
He is preparing to die, and you are his hand.
You are very alive, and he has plans for you.

> Two by two he'll send you all out,
> four feet of peace between you:
> seventy-two lambs amongst teeming wolves,
> and you will receive your due.

> Heal where you may, as we have done
> and bring word of the Kingdom,
> for the day of judgment is near
> and those who reject us reject him, too.

What will they say when *he's* gone, when *we're* gone?
He was a *kind* man? He was a *wise* man, a moral teacher?
We were purpose-driven, with seven highly-effective habits?
Who's going to be the one to set them all straight?

You.   ☦

Disciple

Neighbors Like These

My neighbor snuck up behind me
And tried to steal my cloak
I said *Here, take my shirt too*
He did, he and his buddies

More, they robbed and beat me
And left me lying in a ditch
This turn-your-other-cheek thing
Is not working out so well for me

Yes, friendly folk are fast disappearing
Neighbors lie outright and worse
God sees violence done to the helpless
And vows to rise to their rescue

But how?

Staggered and fallen and waiting to die
I am finished, in final decline
I am interred in my own ditch
Ignored by priests and pastors-by

Have mercy on me in my sorrow
Snatch me back from the maw of death
I long to praise you in the gates of Jericho
To sing of how you have saved me

Lord, deliver me *by* my enemies
I have no hope but this
For I too remain your foe
And my neighbors love me as I love myself   ⊕

Dialogue 2

Lord, who will be allowed into your presence
when you come into your own upon Zion?

How do you read Scripture?

Those who refuse to gossip
   or harm their neighbors
   or speak evil of their friends;
Those who despise sinners
   and honor the faithful
   and keep their word;
Those who cannot be bribed for false witness.

I have observed all this instruction
and even lend money interest-free!

            Can the spirit of God
               be captured in a list?
            A flagrant sinner
               may break your heart
            but mercy and grace
               can mend what breaks.
            Can you uphold the law and sling stones
               with the same hand?
            Is there room in your heart
               to both despise and love?
            If not, which do you suppose
               will win the day?   ☦

What I Want for You

You came to my window at midnight
    asking for snakes.
I'm sorry, but I have no snakes for you.
    I am not sleeping
but no, I have no snakes for you.

You came to my window at one
    asking for scorpions.
I'm sorry, but I have no scorpions for you.
    I am still not sleeping
but no, there are no scorpions to be had.

You came to my window at two
    asking for stones.
I'm sorry, but I have no stones for you.
    I am awake as awake can be
but don't you want something better than stones?

You came to my window at three
    asking for fish.
I'm sorry, but I don't have fish for you.
    I do not drowse at that hour
but you'll just have to wait if you want fish.

You came to my window at four
    asking for an egg.
That might lead to something
    as I fire my ovens.
But don't scorpions hatch from eggs?

You came to my window at five
    asking for bread.
Ah! Now there is something I am about
    and I will be baking soon.
But no bread, no—not yet.

You came to my window at six
    again asking for bread.
I admire your persistence, but no—
    my hands are in the dough.
Are you only concerned about yourself?

You came to my window throughout the day
    seeking bread for your guests.
When the baking was done I gave you a basket
    and I was happy to do so.
But when will it dawn on you to ask for more?

You don't darken my door at any hour
    asking for the gift of my spirit
which is all I have ever wanted for you—
    not eggs or fish or snakes or scorpions.
But to everyone who asks, I give—without delay.

Then when you come to my door at midnight
    and ask for bread
I will say, *Yes—Come in and join me!*
    You see, the door has always been open
and you and I shall share a loaf, and the cup.   ☦

Dear Diary

I am not a collector of histories
They do not wedge in my mind
The way gills catch in a net

What would I tell you ten years from now
About what I saw today?
What can I tell you now?

Jesus cast a demon out of a mute
And the man regained his tongue
Of that much I am fairly certain

But the specifics of one healing
The variations of the Master's aphorisms
Blend one into another and I lose them

A week from now could I tell you
If this man (or another) was also blind
Or if he was healed at noon or dusk?

Could I tell you if we were in Judea
Or by a lakeshore somewhere in Galilee?
Did Jesus use the word "Beelzebul" or "Satan"?

Why does it matter so to you
You damned idolator of words?
The devil is in the details, they say—and are right

If a story falls in the forest
But I do not describe its arc accurately
Does that mean it never happened?

Woe to you who file facts away in boxes
Pressed and dried like faded blossoms
Or stuck with pins like moths and beetles

Woe to you who think more
Of mastering the details of a story
Than yielding your soul to the Master

Woe to you who'd rather know if Jesus said
He who is not with me or *He who is not against us*
Than look to see where your own feet stand

Let those who have eyes read
My journal is not the good news
My words will never save anyone   ☦

So It Begins

A righteous storm you say is coming,
a maelstrom of fire and judgment.
The strongest among us will burn like straw
and our own evil deeds will spark the blaze.

Much will be expected you say
and the inheritance divided.
But how do I judge what is right
to settle with my enemy before they drag me away?

What spirit can I hope to fall upon me?
What will I say when I am clapped in chains?
Who will stand for me in my defense?
Will fine words spill from my lips?

Tell me, yes, tell me
where will these hordes be
who now tread on themselves
to crowd in and listen?

Will I turn my face away from you
and will angels turn away from me?
If I be once, twice, three times a traitor
then yes, by all means cut me down.

And may the flame
             never
                be
                   quenched.   ✛

Mutineers

Eighteen years with crick in 'er back
   Woe ho ho and a wineskin o' pain
Drink nor the de'il will cut no one slack
   Woe ho ho and a wineskin o' pain

Wait we for Monday to make 'er spine straight?
   Honor we the Lord's Day yet kowtow to hate?
List'ning to Pharisees can drive ye insane
   Woe ho ho and a lifetime o' pain

Eyes wide ope' without seeing a thing
   Woe ho ho and a lifetime o' pain
'Twasn't no sin this suff'ring did bring
   Woe ho ho and a lifetime o' pain

Wait 'til tomorrow to give this man sight?
   Slice off my nose my own face to spite?
No, I am sorry—we shall not refrain
   Drink we no more from yr. flagon o' pain

Unleash yr. ox and lead him away
   Fodder yr. ass and heed what he bray
Do what is right and break free this day
   No, no mo' woe—make an end to the pain   ☦

The Impastor

I am a nail in the door of the fold
entombed in cypress from before my time
dead and rusty, I go neither in nor out

I am the missing stone at the gap in the wall
I watch as the thief passes within
I lie in the path and sheep tumble over me

I am a wolf in the guise of a ram
I see the ewes bunching as they strain at the gate
and press myself among them

I am the bramble that catches the wool
I am the thorn that infects the hoof
I am the pink that makes the eye run

I am no shepherd
I am a hireling
who runs at the squeak of danger

where is my flock?
who heeds my voice?
whose needs do I satisfy?

I roam along troubled waters
at the foot of desolate barrens
I destroy the soul

Yes, I am but a lamb
enthralled by an echo
the sound of my own voice

⊕

In the Valley of Vision

Blessed is he who comes in the name of the Lord.
The time came for the nail to be removed.

As I made my way to the feast
an alarm came from the tower watchman
Night is coming and chariots are in the gates
but I dast not ignore my Lord's summons

The table was broad and set for a host
Some had come to be healed or forgiven
some because they were poor and hungry
I had been invited to observe and learn

A crowd jostled for position at the table's head
while my usual place of false humility
at the table's foot was already eagerly filled
So I looked and found my assigned seat

My Lord had prepared a table for me
in the immediate vicinity of my enemy

　　And then I saw

The table had not been prepared for me
but for my enemy, as an honored guest
He was no longer assailing the city's gates
but invited by my Lord to the table's head

　　And then I saw further

The table was not a table, but a door
a narrow door that when opened
led not downward but to an ascending ladder
So I stood and grasped the handle

A psalm of destruction died on my lips
as I turned to my enemy and said

After you.   ☦

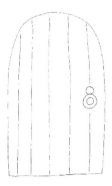

Behold the Lamb

Behold the lamb,
The lamb which is to be slain.

Not twelve days hence bore I
this lamb upon my shoulder,
mud and sweat leaching past my brow,
the lamb's wool matted and bloody.

Father did not need bid me seek:
I gladly left the ninety and nine
in the safety of the shelt'ring fold
while I went in search of the stray.

I pushed through brambles upon the scarp;
my feet trod well past the narrow path;
I dangled from shrubs to grasp the nape
while my brother drank with whores.

And when I returned I cried aloud
Found is the sheep who thrice was lost!
I shared my joy with the household slaves,
yea, for the third time in as many days.

And now the stubborn lamb for which I toiled
shall preparèd be for feasting,
a savory meal for the honored guest:
my brother returned from his debauch.

I have counted the cost of obedience.
It is a burden I simply cannot bear

•

Lord, what must I do to be saved?

What does the good news say to you?

Love your enemy, and pray
for those who persecute you.
I have done all these things.

Even the godless man
may find it in his heart
to forgive a stranger,
enemy though he be.
What credit is it to you
if you do the same?

How then can I be saved?

Forgive your brother,
on whom the Father
lavishes so much mercy.
For hate of the brother
you begrudge and despise
may be your greatest foe.

☦

One Helluva Tip

Let's say a man owns 10,000 sheep.
What is the loss of a single lamb to him?
What is the loss of just ten
in any given year?

The shrewd shepherd knows
how to make two or more
just disappear.
The owner won't give them a second thought.

He's got bigger fish to fry,
as it were,
other flocks to acquire.
The loss of one just doesn't matter.

Let's say a man owns a thousand;
it just won't do to have ten
go "astray."
Best content yourself with one.

But if a man owns one hundred
he will search high and low
for just a single lost lamb.
Don't be caught red-handed.

The man who has just one
is to be pitied most of all
for the loss of his sheep matters.
It matters a great deal.

Aspire, then, to own a flock of 10,000
or to work for the man who does.
Forget about what you ought to do.
Just do what makes sense.

This is sound advice.
Everyone here agrees.
Even my boss commends me.

If only it just weren't so damned hot.   ⊕

What Happens Next

He stands before the tomb
And he weeps

Not for the dead
Nor for the grieving
But because he knew this would happen
And that the Father had willed it

He knew that Lazarus would die
Even before he fell ill
Two days' delay, three days...
What would it matter?

He knew, and he knows
Something great
Is about to happen
As he weeps

And what shall we say
When it comes to pass?
Shall we contrive a celebration
In verbal gymnastics?

> Marvel that he makes all things known?
> Declare that Lazarus is now a known creation
> That the Lord's mercies are known each mourning
> That a known life has now begun?

No. He knew this was going to happen
And whatever next befalls
That is miracle enough
And I am terrified

Jesus stands before the tomb
And he weeps

What else does he know?
What else does he know... about me?

mistaken

his, no ordinary life
gaze on him too long—he vanishes like a star
he lives the truth, lives it slant

his, no ordinary death
flashing in the east, seen in the west—like lightning
the son goes glorious, silent

where be we when he's called home
resting abed—grinding the corn—sowing the field
or warming hands round a fire

☦

II Hezekiah

Who will hear these lessons from the past?
Who will acknowledge the ruin that awaits?

    I asked, "What must I do to be saved?"
      I have always been faithful.
    I have served Jehovah single-mindedly
      Always doing what pleases him.

    "Set your affairs in order," replied my Lord,
      "For this sickness is your undoing."
    I cried, "It is but the summer of my life
      And I may as well be dead!"
    The sum of my work was blown away
      Like a shepherd's tent in a storm.
    Devastated, I chattered like a swallow
      And moaned like a mourning dove.
    For what could I say in response?
      Jehovah himself has afflicted me with wealth.
    My illness is but blessing and prosperity:
      The last shall be first, and the first... lost.
    I could only walk humbly away
      To bear the burden I have been given.

    But the Lord heard my cries and called,
      "You have not expired yet; come, follow me."
    This message from the Master is good;
      My sickness has not destroyed me.
    I may finish my barns and empty them later;
      They may even be sacked by strangers.
    My son may be enslaved and sold as a eunuch,
      Even, perhaps, become one by choice.

But the dead cannot praise Jehovah.
   They cannot raise their voices in hope.
As I still live, for years—even fifteen—
   Surely peace and security shall follow me.

Think on it! The Lord is always eager to save.
   He will be waiting when I am ready.

The rich are aflame and refuse understanding.
They are consumed and do not heed the lesson.   ☦

Long Suffering

The kingdom of heaven is like a healer
Who went out early in the morning
Seeking those in need of aid

He came to the pool of Siloam
Stirring the waters for those in pain
He went out again at about the third hour
And found a man paralyzed
He caused him to walk once more
Sending him on his way
Again he went out at the sixth hour
And met a woman who had bled for twelve years
A woman healed at the touch of his cloak
About the eleventh hour he went out
And mixing mud with dust and saliva
Caused a man born blind to see

When evening came he called his servant
Saying, "What has become of those I touched?"
"Some are with us now, my Lord," said he
"While some have returned to their old lives
Some have presented themselves at the temple
And others have gone to their homes praising your name"

When night fell the healer heard a voice
A prayer from a tent pitched outside the house
"Lord, when will this suffering end?" cried a man
"My wife lies in my arms tonight
As she has lo these twenty years
When will you show mercy?
Her bones are like dry twigs
And snap when she but breathes
Her appetite has left her entirely
Choice foods are but gall and wormwood

Her energy is all but gone
And she succumbs to sleep at mid-day
Yet her spirit has not forsaken you
Still she lives in hope of rebirth
Will you not hear her pleas?"

The healer answered, rose and went to the woman
"Child, do you feel that I am doing you wrong
Because I have sought out others to heal?
Yes, you have your afflictions
But my desire for the lame and the leprous
Is the same as my desire for you
Would it not be as right to heal tomorrow
As to make you whole today?
Would deliverance in a fortnight suffice?
What promise of restoration will you accept?
Can you believe that perseverance serves me too?
Might you walk in pain until I call you home
Or do you begrudge those whom I have touched?
Is your eye envious because I am generous?"

So the last shall be first, and the first last.   ⳨

Hang it All

Wake up, wake up, O Jerusalem
For you shall drink the cup of God's fury
You shall drain the cask of terror
Tipping out its very last bitter dregs

The king has returned from a distant land
And you have squandered what he entrusted
You have hidden riches in your neighbor's field
And buried your heads in your own

Your God is a hard master, as you know
He takes up what others lay down
He reaps where he has not sown
Harvesting richly what others dare to grow

So wake up, wake up, O Zion
Prepare for plunder, to be stripped bare
What you have long taken for granted
He will bequeath to the oppressed and destitute

Take your place in the dust, City of David
For this is what the Lord has spoken
I send you once again into disgrace and exile
And I have no further plans to redeem you

Wail, for the kingdom is coming upon you
And calamity rides in the prince's train
Who is left to sympathize with you?
Who now will give comfort or aid?

Yes, Zaccheus is a squat little man
    A tax-collector/cheat is he
We'll string him up from a sycamore tree
    An example for all to see

Or not

What the hell happened there, anyway?   ☦

12 Days Uncaritas

The day before Passover Jesus said to feed
The poor who are always with me

Two days before Passover Jesus said to feed
Two beggars blind
And the poor who are always with me

Three days before Passover Jesus said to feed
Three ailing kids
A pair of beggars blind
And the poor who are always with me

Four days before Passover Jesus said to feed
Four thousand mouths
Three ailing kids
Blinded beggars twain
And the poor who are always with me

Five days before Passover Jesus said to feed
Five thousand mouths
Four thousand more
Three ailing kids
Two beggars blind
And the poor who are always with me

Six days before Passover Jesus said to feed
Six men on pallets
Five thousand mouths
Four thousand more
Three ailing kids
A brace of beggars blind
And the poor who are always with me

Seven days 'fore Passover Jesus said to feed
Seven tainted harlots
Six men on sick beds
Five thousand mouths
Four thousand more
Three ailing kids
A deuce of beggars blind
And the poor who are always with me

Eight days before Passover Jesus said to feed
Eight lame men limping
Seven tainted harlots
Six sickly sick men
Five thousand mouths
Four thousand more
Three ailing kids
A couple beggars blind
And the poor who are always with me

Nine days before Passover Jesus said to feed
Nine lepers pleading
Eight lame men limping
Seven harlots pimping
Six sickly sick men
Five thousand mouths
Four thousand more
Three ailing kids
Blinded beggars twain
And the poor who are always with me

Ten days before Passover Jesus said to feed
Ten lepers pleading
Nine of them leaving
Eight lame men gimping
Seven harlots pimping
Six men a-sicking
Five thousand mouths

Four thousand more
Three dying kids
Beggars one and two
And the poor who are always with me

Eleven days 'fore Passover Jesus said to feed
Eleven taxing taxmen
Ten lepers pleading
Nine of them leaving
Eight lame men gimping
Seven harlots pimping
Six men a-sicking
Five thousand mouths
Four thousand more
Three dying kids
Two beggars blind
And the poor who are always with me

Twelve days before Passover Jesus said to feed
All twelve disciples
Eleven taxmen taxing
Ten lepers pleading
Nine ingrates leaving
Eight gimps a-limping
Seven pimps a-pimping
Six sick men sicking
Five thousand mouths
Four thousand whores
Three dead kids
Those two sightless dudes—
Yes, the poor who are always—always—with *me!*   ☦

Bound for Glory

Lift up your heads, O ye gates!
Be lifted up, ye ancient doors,
For the King of Glory is coming in!

Who is this king, the King of Glory?
The Lord, strong and mighty,
The Lord, mighty in battle!

Our time has come, the time to arise.
We lay our cloaks in his path
That the King's colt might not touch earth.

Blessed are we who come in the train of the Lord!
My liege has need of me, and I know what I must do.
I shall not remain silent; this stone shall certainly cry out.
I shall bear fruit without ceasing, both in and out of season.

He shall have no cause to rebuke or curse.

His might breaks through like the dawn!
Our champion leads in the van
With the glory of the Lord behind—

Yes, the glory of the Lord trails behind.   ☦

I Don't Want to Go to Jerusalem

A Song of Cowardice

I don't want my temples cleansed
I know what that means
I don't want to rock the boat,
Bite the hand that feeds my bloat

I don't want to make a scene,
Dare to take a stand—
Say out loud that Christ is King,
Pay the price such 'tention brings

I don't want my temples cleansed
I don't have the means
I don't want to wither figs
Move my mountains, much less twigs

I won't have my wounds be healed
'Gardless how they pain
I don't want my eyes to see,
Yield my hardened heart to thee

Jesus, you just ask too much
See
      Spot
         Run   ☦

Truth to Power

I wait at the gate as they talk.
Yentas have nothing on scribes and rabbis
prating endlessly about petty details.
Knotted behind me on the courtyard steps,
they pepper the young teacher
with baited queries about coinage and tribute.
Here in Herod's temple, of all places.

I stay in the gate and I watch
as the Levite carrying pigeons—
yea, birds I bought with temple coin—
delivereth them to the vested priest.
Their enflamed blood rendreth me clean.
Do these wranglers of words behind
not see the cold irony of their banter?
Like blood-soaked priests they wring the heads
from bandied words and scatter their entrails,
missing the point entirely.

I turn from the gate as I mock.
The law telleth me that I am unclean
66 days after birthing mine now-fatherless child.
I must needs bring a lamb to sacrifice,
which maketh me pure in the eyes of men—
which maketh me pure in the eyes of men!
But the law alloweth the poor to substitute birds,
birds I must purchase with temple coin,
coin birthed only from Roman coin: Tell me,
is that rendering to God what is God's?
The temple is taxing in its own rite—
why do ye scribes wish to avoid Rome's?
What would ye do with the coin ye save?
Care for widows whose scant Roman coin
ye are only too eager to change?

Or wouldst thou purchase more offerings
to pay for thine own many-splendored sins?
There, I have said too much.

I depart from the gate as they gawk,
cross 'neath the lampstand's shade
and approach the Treasury as they natter.
There is so little left that I can do.
I take what remaineth to me,
Two tiny Roman coins—yea, Roman—
and I drop them into the box.
They chime shrilly as they disappear.
What, now, will the learnèd do with that?   ☩

Not Taken

A housecat writhes
On my lap as I write
Its tongue reels out
Again, and again
As its head bobs over its coat

The cat does not clean
Because it likes the taste of fur
Were that the case
The cat would clean more
Than it sleeps or eats or purrs

No, the cat savors washing
Because of what follows
Because of what is left behind
In spite of the bad taste
The sheen, the gleam, all things made new

Watch a cat gnaw
As it purges its hind claws
The vicious joy in the effort
The fiery passion for purity
Sharp teeth taking away the dirt

    So it was in the days of Noah
    So it was later in Sodom
    So it was at the sack of Samaria, and of Zion
    So it will be when the Son of Man comes
    O, to be left behind

Oh, to be left behind!   ☦

The Shoes of a Fisherman

I rise each day with anger
Gird my loins with her, bathe with her, and bed her down
I dare not give her to God

If I can't keep pace with peace
How on Earth do I expect to soar with eagles
How in Hell walk like Jesus?

The shoes of the carpenter
Limn a path toward a Roman tree—O pray for him
Yes, pray for him, and for me

✠

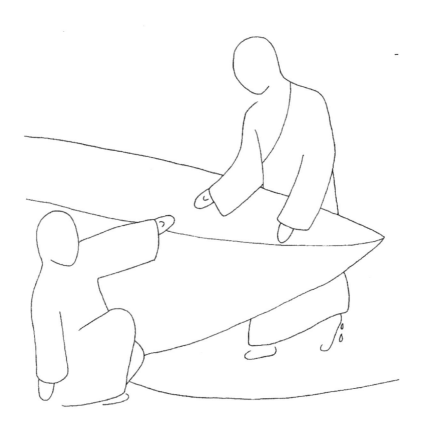

I.t I.s I

Words are not
the only things
to fail at times
such as these.

What would you say
If a stranger came to your door
Saying, *I see your servant carries water*
Our master sends you word
Show us the room you have prepared
That we may break bread inside

Do you want to be known so deeply
Are your thoughts so pure your mind would bid
Welcome, make yourself at home

What would you say
When told that Satan sifts your soul
When told that you will turn away
Three times 'fore break of day
When your two-faced heart
Dips bread with one Lord and Master

Would you say *never*
I would sooner die
Would you lie
Through your gnashing teeth

What can you say
When you've run away
When you've mastered
Your abandon in the garden
When you recall the words
I shall see you again

How can you face that thought
Does courage or gorge rise anew

Yes, you see him again
Even look into his eyes
And still you turn away
And turn away
Turn, turn away

Betrayal punctuates the night

What do you say
When courage fails
When your brags of allegiance
Hang flaccid and empty

Lesser love has no man than this

Were you there
When they crucified our Lord
I wouldn't know

But the Paraclete is with me
Whispering in my ear
This heinous crime is yours
Own it
You are not a fisher of men
You are not even a poor shepherd

You are nothing
You are lost

I want to vanish
Yet the question marks
My soul, remains

How do you let go
Oh, how do I let it go?

In Tongues Unknown

In Hebrew we have three words for sin.

Peter, why did you deny me? Jesus asked.
I honestly didn't know what I was doing, I protested.
You know I have the greatest affection for you.

And the second time? He pressed.
That was more a sin of omission, I demurred.
I didn't know what else to do.
But you know I love you like a brother.

But the third time, Peter, what of that?
I chose wrong deliberately, Master.
My heart was hard, and I was ashamed.
Still, I assure you that my love
knows no bounds.

I shall never feed His flock
until my tongue finds five words for faith
and twelve terms for hope,
until I step out of the tentative quiet
between the empty tomb and the future,
between miracles past and those yet to be.

Until this is all no longer Greek to me.   ☦

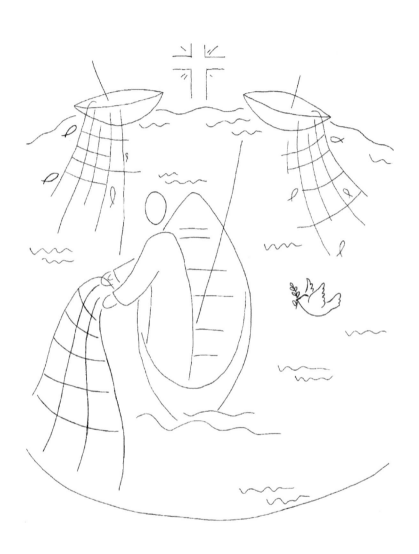

Epilogue: Hell or High Water

I choose the voyage prepared
The course set in the presence of my enemies
Yes, I choose the Master's craft

I've no need to walk on waves
I wade through shallows, swing my foot over the rail
Living water drips from toes

I say come, Holy Spirit
Fill the sails and head for the deep—let's start fishing
There are many mouths to feed.

☦

Acknowledgments

The contents of this volume were written between 2013 and 2017, during which time my late wife Jenn was reconciling herself to an early death. Over those years, as we were practicing the disciplines of Spiritual Formation as learned in retreats through Christian Formation & Direction Ministries (CFDM) Northwest, I immersed myself in an intensive "lectio divinia" with the NASB Thomas/Gundry *Harmony of the Gospels*, beginning with Peter's first encounter with Jesus of Nazareth. These poems immediately began to pour forth.

But this project really began much, much earlier. In 1992, theater colleague Melanie Calderwood recruited me to play the part of Saint Peter in a production of the play *This Rock*. The setting of the one-act is the day after Jesus' execution, and Peter contemplates suicide over his betrayal of his master. Preparation for the role marked my first true immersion in Scripture; and as I began to really get inside Simon Peter's head, I began to understand its similarity to my own. I instinctively recoiled from the emotion of the role in rehearsals, but the flood broke during the single Good Friday performance. I could not stop sobbing for close to half an hour after curtain. The "sense memory" I had developed for Simon Peter made me feel that I, as Peter, had actually been in Jesus' presence and received his unmerited grace. The experience taught me that close encounters with Scripture can produce profound spiritual effects—a lesson that I carried into Dramatic Insights Ministries, which I led from 1993 through 2002.

Group Spiritual Direction with CFDM reawakened memories of Peter's psyche. I knew that this was a spiritual well which I needed to draw from more thoroughly.

So *The Gospel of Doubt* is a cycle of poems that has been nearly thirty years in the making.

First and foremost I must acknowledge the role of God's Spirit in leading me through all of this—and the mighty power of Jesus' words and the Gospels themselves. Right behind the Trinity is Jenn herself, who sat at my side as I wrote every one of these words—and heard every one of them read aloud for the first time. The four of them are now truly one, and thick as thieves.

Next, I am indebted to Shelly Morse, who introduced Jenn (and then me) to CFDM, and to both her and Clint Morse for being companions with us through the two nine-month cohorts that followed. Boni Piper and Terry Tripp, through their excellent spiritual leadership, guided Jenn and me through the very painful process of fully accepting God's love so that we could love ourselves, for the sake of others. Sara Wagner, as my Group Spiritual Direction leader, opened me up to the possibilities and power of the *lectio divina* and guided imagery.

In addition to Melanie Calderwood, I also thank my community theater companions Michelle Tuck and Judy Schwanke, as well as my core drama ministry partners Michael Brunk, Brenda Dyrdahl, Lyla Moreland, George Rosok, and Dave Stark, for their collaboration and support through my initial forays into persona literature.

Nonetheless, these words would not have been written without the spiritually nurturing and creatively supportive environment at Harambee Church in Renton. A special thanks to Pastor John Prince for his leadership and companionship there.

Two very spiritually-minded literary friends also opened their minds and hearts to me during the years of the writing, and greatly influenced the words which wound up on the page: Fiona Micheli and Monique Bos. Thanks to you both, deeply.

Finally, I thank the Confluence Poets for their immediate and warm embrace upon my arrival in the Methow valley, and Subhaga Crystal Bacon in particular for her friendship and encouragement of this project.

About the Author

Greg Wright is a pastor, technology consultant, lecturer, film critic, and writer who taught literature, film, and theater while Writer in Residence at Puget Sound Christian College. Managing Editor of HollywoodJesus.com from 2000-2012, he is the author and editor of many scholarly works, including *Two Roads Through Narnia*, *Tolkien in Perspective*, *Peter Jackson in Perspective*, and *The Da Vinci Code Adventure*. Under the pen name W. John MacGregor, he has published the novels *West of the Gospel* and the forthcoming *Early Winters*. His published plays include *Homecoming*, *Beasley's Christmas Party* (adapted from the book of the same title and *Ramsey Milholland*, both by Booth Tarkington), and a three-act adaptation of William Shakespeare's *Measure for Measure*.

In 2019 he joined the Methow Valley's Confluence Poets. His poems have appeared in *The Shrub-Steppe Poetry Journal* and *Whispers of Wenatchee*. *The Gospel of Doubt* is his first published collection.

Colophon

The Gospel of Doubt by Greg Wright
was set in Garamond by Methow Press.
The cover design is by Greg Wright.
The cover and interior art was commissioned from
Zoe Prince.
Manufactured by LightningSource, LaVergne, Tennessee.